An I Can Read Book™

W9-BLS-817

STUART LITTLE™

Stuart Sets Sail

story by Susan Hill

pictures by Lydia Halverson

HarperCollins*Publishers*

Stuart Sets Sail
TM & © 2001 by Columbia Pictures Industries, Inc. All Rights Reserved
Story by Susan Hill
Illustrations by Lydia Halverson
Printed in the U.S.A. All rights reserved.
www.harperchildrens.com

Library of Congress Cataloging-in-Publication Data
Hill, Susan.
    Stuart sets sail / by Susan Hill ; pictures by Lydia Halverson.
        p.   cm.
Summary: When Stuart Little and his family go for a picnic at a lake, he has several
adventures as he tries to sail across the lake on George's sailboat.
    ISBN 0-06-029537-6 — ISBN 0-06-029633-X (lib. bdg.) — ISBN 0-06-444302-7 (pbk.)
    [1. Mice—Fiction. 2. Boats and boating—Fiction.] I. Halverson, Lydia, ill. II. Title.
PZ7.H5574 Sv 2001   00-059697
[E]—dc21

                              4   5   6   7   8   9   10
                                              ❖
                                      First Edition

Stuart Sets Sail

TO LAKE
3 miles

One sunny day,

Stuart Little and his family

drove to a lake in the country.

Mr. Little carried the picnic basket.

Mrs. Little carried the blanket.

George carried his boat, the *Wasp*.

Stuart carried dessert.

"What a big lake," said Stuart.

"I can't wait to sail across it!"

"That sounds like fun, Stuart,"
said Mrs. Little, "but come back
before the sun hits the tops
of those trees.
We want to be home
before it gets dark."

Stuart set sail.

The wind blew softly.

Suddenly Stuart heard

SPLISH! SPLASH!

11

"It's a whale!" Stuart yelled.

"No, I'm just a fish
with a whale of a problem.
I have a hook stuck in my lip!"
said the fish.

"I can help you," said Stuart.

He pulled the hook out.

"Thank you!" cried the fish.

"You are welcome," said Stuart.

The fish swam away.

Stuart looked up.

The sun had moved closer to the trees.

"I still have time

to cross the lake," said Stuart.

The wind picked up.

"Whooee!" shouted Stuart.

"I will be at the other side

of the lake soon!"

BUMP!

The *Wasp* ran into a rock.

"Where did that rock come from?"

asked Stuart.

He stepped onto the rock

to check for leaks in the *Wasp*.

Suddenly the rock began to move.

"Whoa!" shouted Stuart.

"Do I look like a rock to you?" it said.

"You look like a turtle, now,"

said Stuart.

"You look like lunch to me!"

snapped the turtle.

Stuart jumped back into the boat.

"Phew!" said Stuart.

"That was close!"

Stuart looked up.

The sun was closer

to the tops of the trees.

"I still have time

to cross the lake," said Stuart.

He sailed on.

21

Suddenly a motorboat sped by.

Big waves tossed the *Wasp*.

Then a large bird flew over the boat.

His wings whipped the sails.

"Having a good time, Sailor?"

called the bird.

"I prefer calmer winds,

if you don't mind!" Stuart shouted.

"Ha-ha." The bird laughed

and flew away.

"That was some storm!" said Stuart.

He looked up.

The sun was very close

to the tops of the trees.

The other side of the lake

was still far away.

"Well," said Stuart,

"it is time to go back."

Stuart turned the *Wasp* around

and sailed back to shore.

"Did you sail to the other side,

Stuart?" asked George.

"No," said Stuart.

"But did you see

all my big adventures?

Did you see the fish,

the rock, and the storm?"

"We didn't see anything, Son,"
Mr. Little said.
"It looked like smooth
sailing from here."

"Oh," Stuart said. "I guess they were only little adventures."

"Adventures come in all sizes, Stuart," said Mrs. Little.

Stuart smiled.

"So does dessert!"